For Janet and my parents.   T.O'B.
For Christopher and Harriet.   M.G.

First published in the United States 1991 by
Dial Books for Young Readers
A Division of Penguin Books USA Inc.
375 Hudson Street
New York, New York 10014

Published in Great Britain by J.M. Dent & Sons Ltd.
Text copyright © 1990 by Margaret Greaves
Pictures copyright © 1990 by Teresa O'Brien
All rights reserved
Printed in Italy
First Edition
N
1 3 5 7 9 10 8 6 4 2

Library of Congress Cataloging in Publication Data
Greaves, Margaret.
Henry's wild morning / by Margaret Greaves; pictures by Teresa O'Brien.
p. cm.
Summary: Henry, the smallest kitten in the litter, pretends he is as big and brave as a tiger.
ISBN 0-8037-0907-2
[1. Cats—Fiction.] I. O'Brien, Teresa, ill. II. Title.
PZ7.G8He 1991 [E]—dc20 90-3554 CIP AC

The art for each picture consists of an ink and watercolor painting,
which is scanner-separated and reproduced in full color.

HENRY'S WILD MORNING

Margaret Greaves

pictures by Teresa O'Brien

Dial Books for Young Readers NEW YORK

Henry was the smallest kitten in the litter, and the only one with stripes. His big brother Joseph and his sisters Dizzy and Tizzy sometimes teased him because he was so little.

As they all grew larger the basket became crowded, and Henry was always the one who got squashed. But he didn't mind. He was a very cheerful kitten.

One morning he woke up feeling
very big and wild. He nipped his
brother's tail.

"I'm a tiger," he said. "A big,
fierce tiger. *You* can't be a tiger.
You've got no stripes."

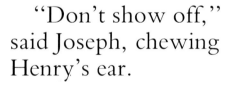

"Don't show off,"
said Joseph, chewing
Henry's ear.

But Henry pranced into the kitchen and ate his breakfast in a very tigerish sort of way.

Then he jumped onto the kitchen table.

Someone had unpacked a shopping basket there. He found several tins and boxes and a big ball of string. He patted the string and it moved.

"Ho!" said Henry. "I'm a tiger and tigers fight things."

He had a very exciting fight with the ball of string until he knocked over two of the tins. They rolled off the table and across the floor. *Crash,* rumble, rumble, *bump.*

Henry was so scared that he rushed out into the garden. Jasper, the dog next door, pushed his nose through the fence.

"Good morning, little Henry. What are you so scared of?"

"I'm *not* scared," hissed the kitten, "and I'm *not* little Henry. I'm a big, fierce, prowling tiger."

He arched his back at Jasper and walked off under some bushes in a prowling sort of way. From there he could see two sparrows pecking on the grass.

He pounced at them, but the sparrows flew up onto the lowest branch of a tree. They perched there, chirping.

"You can't catch us," cheeped one of them.

"You're only a kitten," cheeped the other.

"No, I'm not," said Henry. "I'm a big, fierce, hunting tiger!"

He started to scramble
up the tree. But the
sparrows flew up to
another branch. Henry
climbed after them,
feeling big and brave.
He had never been so
high before.

He had nearly reached the sparrows when they flew almost to the top of the tree. They flirted their wings and chirped at him noisily.

"You can't climb this high. You're too small."

"No, I'm not," said Henry. "I'm a big, fierce tiger."

He went on climbing. But when he was very close, the sparrows cheeped at him and flew down to the grass again.

Henry looked down at them. Suddenly he saw that the ground was very, very far away. And his branch was thin and very wobbly. He forgot about being a tiger.

"Help! Help!" he mewed. "I'm stuck. I'm slipping! Oh help!"

His mother heard him and ran to the bottom of the tree. "You silly little kitten!" she said. "Now listen. It's hard to climb down backward. You must turn around."

"Can't," wailed Henry.

Joseph, Dizzy, and Tizzy came to see what was happening.

"Oooh!" squeaked his sisters. "Look where you are! You are *brave,* Henry."

That made him feel better, but he still couldn't turn around.

"It's easy," said Joseph, who had never climbed so high. "Move your left front paw to the left and your right back paw to the right."

Henry nervously moved one paw, then stopped to think.
Which was his right paw and which was his left?
He never could remember.

"And don't look down," warned his mother.
"Henry, *don't look down!*"

She was too late. Henry had already looked down and
it made him feel quite dizzy. He was still confused about
his paws.

Swish! Rustle, crackle, *plop!*
He had lost his balance and
came falling through the
branches in a shower of leaves
and twigs.

The others rushed to see if he was hurt, but Henry scrambled up and shook himself.

"Did you see?" he squeaked. "I climbed *really* high. Higher than Joseph has, didn't I? I'm a big, fierce tiger."
He was so excited that he tried to scramble up the tree again.

But his mother grabbed him firmly by the scruff of his neck. "You're *not* a big, fierce tiger," she said, shaking him gently, "and you're going straight to your basket."

Henry was quite glad to snuggle down.
Being a tiger was very tiring.

"But I did climb high, didn't I?" he said to his mother.
"Yes, you did, dear," said his mother kindly.

But Henry didn't hear her. He was fast asleep.
And in his dreams he was the biggest and
fiercest tiger in the jungle.